CHRISTMAS
FOR
FLUTE & GUITAR

JERRY WILLARD

flute

Amsco Publications
New York/London/Sydney/Cologne

Contents

O Come, All Ye Faithful

Latin: John F. Wade, 1711–1786   John F. Wade's *Cantus Diversi*, 1751   Translation: Frederick Oakely, 1802–1880, and others

Silent Night

Joseph Mohr, 1792–1848
Translation: John F. Young, 1820–1885, and others

Franz Gruber, 1787–1863

Ending for repeat

Final ending

Coventry Carol

Robert Croo's *Pageant of the Shearmen and Tailors*, 1534

Original tune of 1591

Introduction or interlude

Refrain

Fine

D.S. al Fine

We Wish You a Merry Christmas

Traditional English carol

The Holly and the Ivy

Traditional English carol

God Rest You Merry, Gentlemen

William Sandy's *Christmas Carols Ancient and Modern, 1833*

Traditional English tune

It Came upon the Midnight Clear

Edward Hamilton Sears, 1810–1876

Richard Storrs Willis, 1819–1900

Deck the Hall

Traditional Welsh carol

What Child Is This?

William C. Dix, 1837–1898

Traditional English tune

Refrain

Down in Yon Forest

Traditional English carol

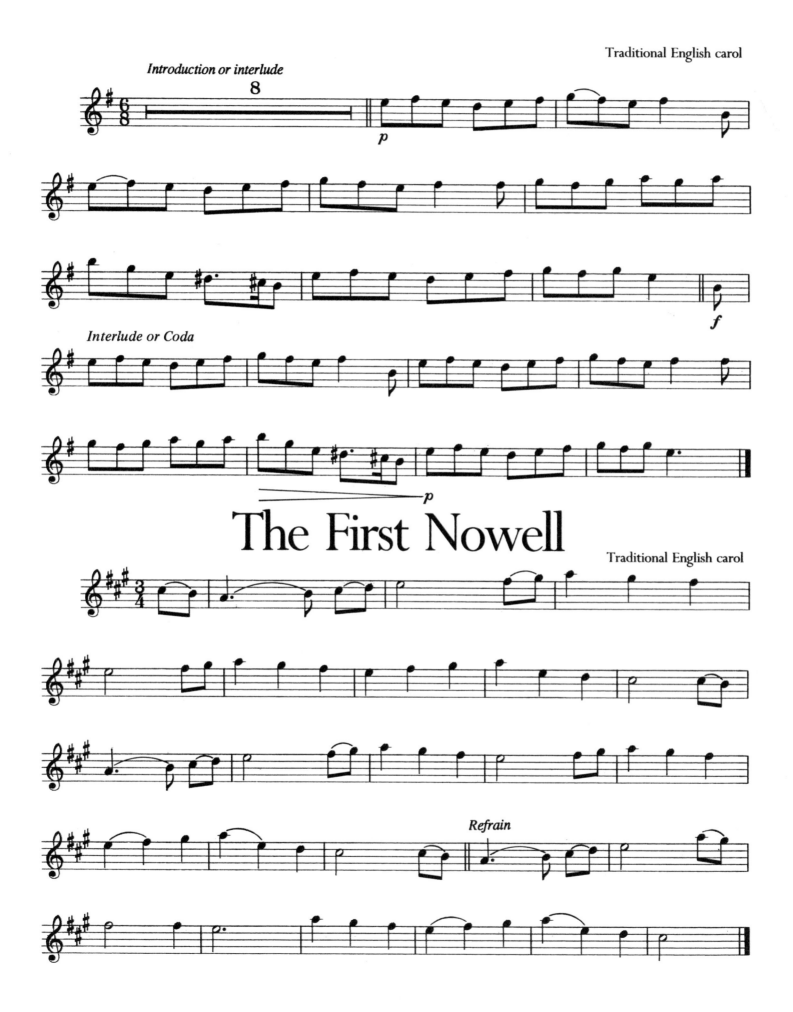

The First Nowell

Traditional English carol

Away in a Manger

first version

Anonymous   William J. Kirkpatrick, 1838–1921

Away in a Manger

second version

Anonymous   James R. Murray, 1841–1905

O Come, O Come, Emmanuel

Latin, 9th century
Translation: John M. Neale, 1818–1866 (stanzas 1,2);
Henry S. Coffin, 1877–1954 (stanzas 3,4)

Adapted from plainsong by Thomas Helmore, 1811–1890

Introduction

We Three Kings

John H. Hopkins, Jr., 1820–1891

A Virgin Most Pure

Traditional English carol

Davies Gilbert's *Some Ancient Christmas Carols,* 1822

Chorus

Good King Wenceslas

John M. Neale, 1818–1866

Theodoricus Petrus of Nyland's *Piae Cantiones*, 1592

Angelus Ad Virginum

(Gabriel to Mary Came)

Introduction or interlude

14th century carol

In Dulci Jubilo

14th century German carol

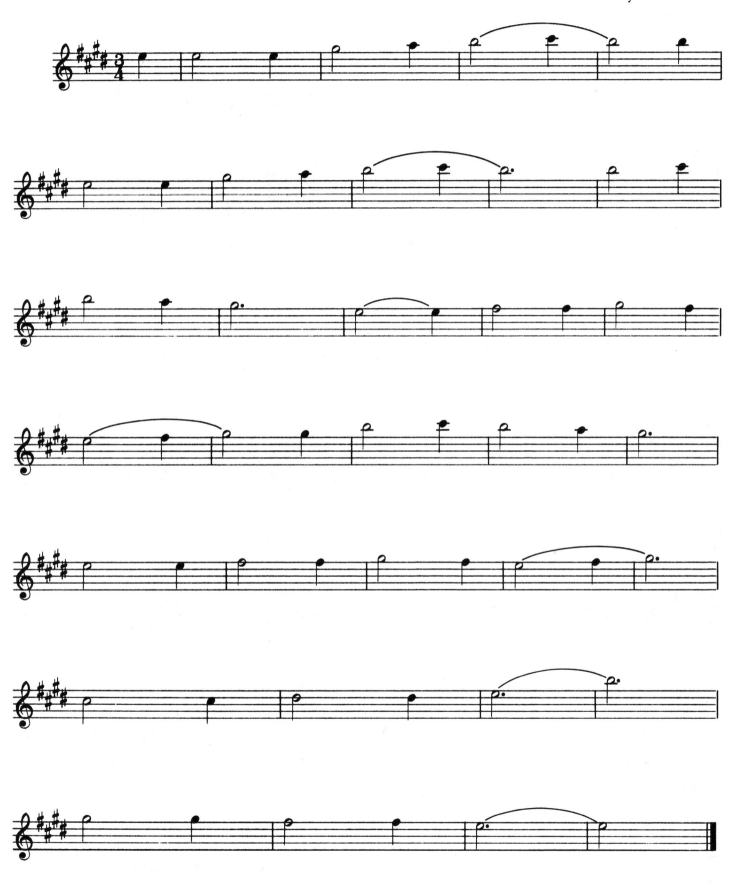

Hark! The Herald Angels Sing

Charles Wesley, 1707–1788

Felix Mendelssohn Bartholdy, 1809–1847

CHRISTMAS
FOR
FLUTE & GUITAR

JERRY WILLARD

Amsco Publications
New York/London/Sydney/Cologne

Edited by Peter Pickow
This book and the arrangements contained herein are
Copyright © 1989 by Amsco Publications,
A Division of Music Sales Corporation, New York, NY.

Order No. AM 67125
US International Standard Book Number: 0.8256.1120.2
UK International Standard Book Number: 0.7119.1241.6

Exclusive Distributors:
Music Sales Corporation
225 Park Avenue South, New York, NY 10003 USA
Music Sales Limited
8/9 Frith Street, London W1V 5TZ England
Music Sales Pty, Limited
120 Rothschild Street, Rosebery, Sydney, NSW 2018, Australia

Printed in the United States of America by
Vicks Lithograph and Printing Corporation

Contents

Preface

A carol is defined as a religious song of joy. Many carols are quite ancient, and quite a few were actually drawn from pagan sources by the early Christian church. Christmas carols may be dramatic, as in "O Come, All Ye Faithful"; narrative, as in "Good King Wenceslas"; or lyrical, as in "Away in a Manger."

For this collection, I have chosen some carols that are famous and some that are not quite so well known. Although the book is designed primarily for the flute and guitar duo, the key for each arrangement has been chosen with the voice in mind as well: All of the carols are eminently singable as written, and the complete lyric for each one has been included. In addition, every attempt has been made to make the arrangements flexible—in some cases through the inclusion of instrumental introductions and interludes—making them suitable to a variety of performance situations.

O Come, All Ye Faithful

Latin: John F. Wade, 1711–1786   John F. Wade's *Cantus Diversi, 1751* Translation: *Frederick Oakely, 1802–1880, and others*

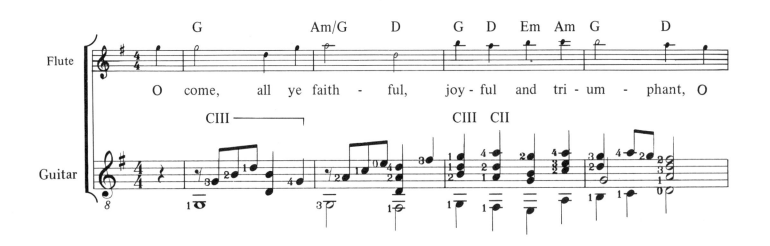

O come, all ye faith - ful, joy - ful and tri - um - phant, O

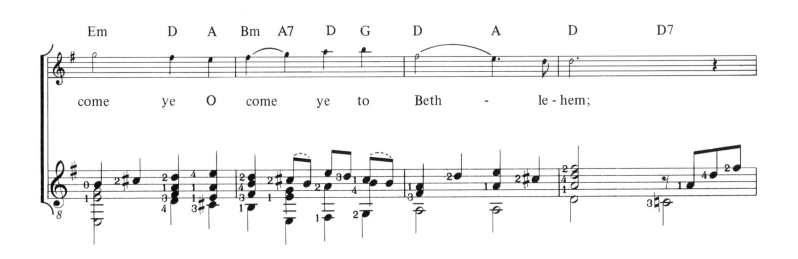

come ye O come ye to Beth - le - hem;

Refrain

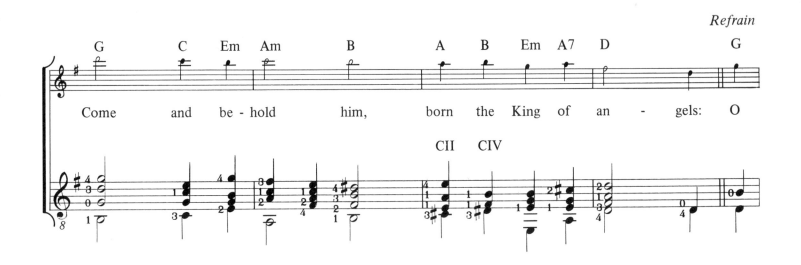

Come and be - hold him, born the King of an - gels: O

1. O come, all ye faithful, joyful and triumphant,
   O come ye, O come ye to Bethlehem;
   Come and behold him, born the King of angels:

   Refrain:
   O come, let us adore him,
   O come, let us adore him,
   O come, let us adore him,
   Christ, the Lord!

2. God of God, Light of Light,
   Lo! he abhors not the virgin's womb:
   Very God, begotten, not created;

   Refrain

3. Sing, choirs of angels, sing in exultation,
   Sing all ye citizens of heaven above!
   Glory to God, all glory in the highest;

   Refrain

4. See how the shepherds, summoned to his cradle,
   Leaving their flocks, draw nigh to gaze;
   We too will thither bend out joyful footsteps;

   Refrain

5. Child, for us sinners poor and in the manger,
   We would embrace thee, with love and awe;
   Who would not love thee, loving us so dearly?

   Refrain

6. Yea, Lord, we greet thee, born this happy morning;
   Jesus, to thee be all glory given;
   Word of the Father, now in flesh appearing;

   Refrain

1. *Adeste fideles, laeti triumphantes,*
   Venite, venite in Bethlehem:
   Natum videte, regem angelorum:

   Refrain:
   Venite, adoremus,
   Venite, adoremus,
   Venite, adoremus,
   Dominum.

2. *Cantet nunc io chorus angelorum,*
   Cantet nunc aula caelestium:
   Gloria in excelsis Deo:

   Refrain

3. *Ergo qui natus die hodierna,*
   Jesu, tibi sit gloria:
   Patris aeterni verbum caro factum:

   Refrain

Silent Night

Joseph Mohr, 1792–1848
Translation: John F. Young, 1820–1885, and others

Franz Gruber, 1787–1863

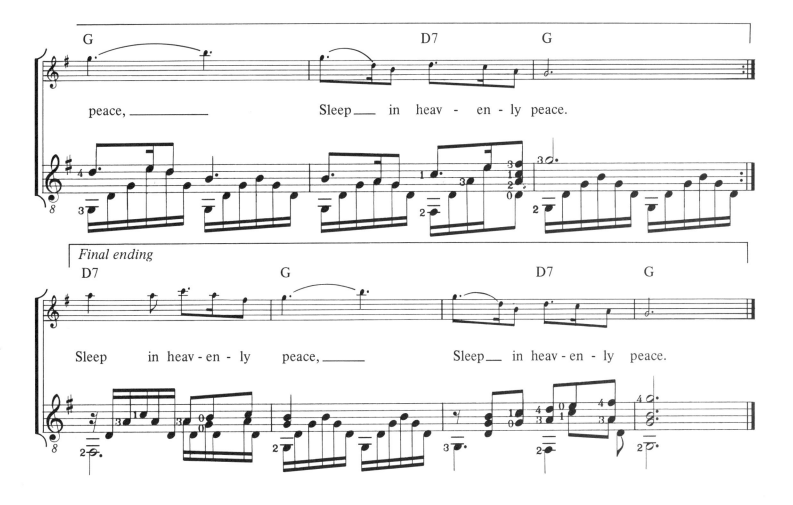

1. Silent night, holy night,
   All is calm, all is bright,
   Round yon virgin mother and child.
   Holy infant so tender and mild,
       Sleep in heavenly peace,
       Sleep in heavenly peace.

2. Silent night, holy night,
   Shepherds quake at the sight,
   Glories stream from heaven afar,
   Heavenly hosts sing alleluia;
       Christ, the Savior, is born!
       Christ, the Savior, is born!

3. Silent night, holy night,
   Son of God, love's pure light,
   Radiant beams from thy holy face,
   With the dawn of redeeming grace;
       Jesus, Lord at thy birth,
       Jesus, Lord at thy birth.

4. Silent night, holy night,
   Wondrous star, lend thy light;
   With the angels let us sing
   Alleluia to our King;
       Christ the Savior is born,
       Christ the Savior is born.

We Wish You a Merry Christmas

Traditional English carol

1. We wish you a merry Christmas,
   We wish you a merry Christmas,
   We wish you a merry Christmas,
   And a happy new year.

   Chorus:
   Good tidings we bring to you and your kin;
   We wish you a merry Christmas and a happy new year.

2. Now bring us some figgy pudding,
   Now bring us some figgy pudding,
   Now bring us some figgy pudding,
   And bring some out here.

   Chorus

3. For we all like figgy pudding,
   We all like figgy pudding,
   We all like figgy pudding,
   So bring some out here.

   Chorus

4. And we won't go until we get some,
   We won't go until we get some,
   We won't go until we get some,
   So bring some out here!

   Chorus

It Came upon the Midnight Clear

Edward Hamilton Sears, 1810–1876

Richard Storrs Willis, 1819–1900

Flute

Guitar

It came up-on — the mid-night clear, That glo-rious song— of old, ——— From an-gels bend-ing near the earth To touch thier harps— of gold: ——— "Peace on the earth,— good will to men, From heav-en's all gra-cious King!" The world in sol-emn still-ness lay, To hear the an-gels sing. ———

1. It came upon the midnight clear,
    That glorious song of old,
    From angels bending near the earth
    To touch their harps of gold:
        "Peace on the earth, good will to men,
        From heaven's all gracious King!"
    The world in solemn stillness lay
    To hear the angels sing.

2. Still through the cloven skies they come
    With peaceful wings unfurled,
    And still their heavenly music floats
    O'er all the weary world;
        Above its sad and lowly plains
        They bend on hovering wing,
    And ever over its Babel sounds
    The blessèd angels sing.

3. Yet with the woes of sin and strife
    The world has suffered long;
    Beneath the angel-strain have rolled
    Two thousand years of wrong;
        And man, at war with man, hears not
        The love-song which they bring.
    O hush the noise, ye men of strife
    And hear the angels sing.

4. And ye, beneath life's crushing load
    Whose forms are bending low,
    Who toil along the climbing way
    With weary steps and slow—
        Look up! for glad and golden hours
        Come swiftly on the wing;
    O rest beside the weary road
    And hear the angels sing.

5. For lo! the days are hastening on,
    By prophet bards foretold,
    When with the ever-circling years
    Comes round the Age of Gold,
        When peace shall over all the earth
        Its ancient splendors fling,
    And the whole world give back the song
    Which now the angels sing.

Deck the Hall

Traditional Welsh carol

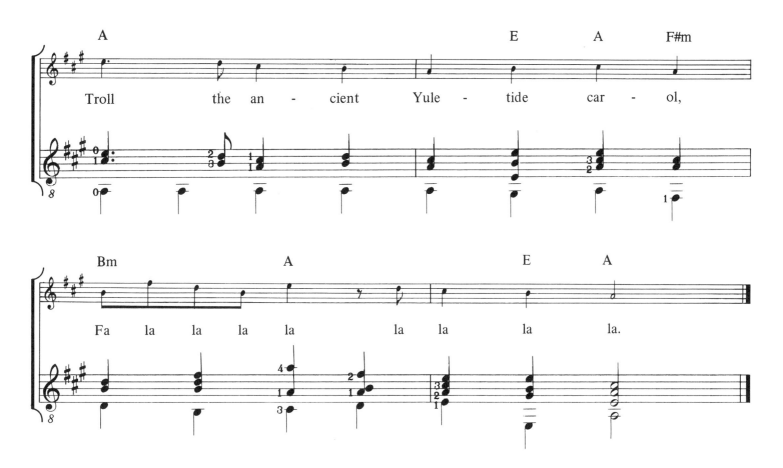

1. Deck the hall with boughs of holly,
   Fa la la la la la la la la.
   Tis the season to be jolly,
   Fa la la la la la la la la.
   Fill the mead cup, drain the barrel,
   Fa la la la la la la la.
   Troll the ancient Yuletide carol,
   Fa la la la la la la la la.

2. See the flowing bowl before us,
   Fa la la la la la la la la.
   Strike the harp and join the chorus,
   Fa la la la la la la la la.
   Follow me in merry measure,
   Fa la la la la la la la.
   While I sing of beauty's treasure,
   Fa la la la la la la la la.

3. Fast away the old year passes,
   Fa la la la la la la la la.
   Hail the new, ye lads and lasses,
   Fa la la la la la la la la.
   Laughing, quaffing, all together,
   Fa la la la la la la la.
   Heedless of the wind and weather,
   Fa la la la la la la la la.

The First Nowell

Traditional English carol

1. The first Nowell the angel did say
   Was to certain poor shepherds in fields as they lay;
   In fields where they lay, keeping their sheep,
   In a cold winter's night that was so deep:

   Refrain:
   Nowell, Nowell, Nowell, Nowell,
   Born is the King of Israel!

2. They lookèd up and saw a star
   Shining in the east, beyond them far;
   And to the earth it gave great light,
   And so it continued both day and night:

   Refrain

3. And by the light of that same star,
   Three wise men came from country far;
   To seek for a king was their intent,
   And to follow the star wheresoever it went:

   Refrain

4. This star drew night to the northwest;
   O'er Bethlehem it took its rest,
   And there it did both stop and stay
   Right over the place where Jesus lay:

   Refrain

5. Then did they know assuredly
   Within the house the King did lie:
   One entered in then for to see
   And found the Babe in poverty:

   Refrain

6. Then entered in those wise men three,
   Fell reverently upon their knee
   And offered there in his presence
   Both gold and myrrh and frankincense:

   Refrain

7. Between an ox-stall and an ass,
   This child truly born he was;
   For want of clothing they did him lay
   All in the manger, among the hay:

   Refrain

8. Then let us all with one accord
   Sing praises to our heavenly Lord
   That hath made heaven and earth of naught
   And with his blood mankind hath bought:

   Refrain

9. If we in our time shall do well,
   We shall be free from death and hell;
   For God hath preparèd for us all
   A resting place in general:

   Refrain

Away in a Manger
first version

Anonymous

William J. Kirkpatrick, 1838–1921

1. Away in a manger, no crib for a bed,
    The little Lord Jesus laid down his sweet head.
    The stars in the bright sky looked down where he lay,
    The little Lord Jesus asleep on the hay.

2. The cattle are lowing, the baby awakes,
    But little Lord Jesus, no crying he makes.
    I love thee, Lord Jesus, look down from the sky,
    And stay by my cradle till morning is nigh.

3. Be near me Lord Jesus, I ask thee to stay
    Close by me forever, and love me, I pray.
    Bless all the dear children in thy tender care,
    And fit us for heaven to live with thee there.

Away in a Manger

second version

Anonymous

James R. Murray, 1841–1905

1. Away in a manger, no crib for a bed,
   The little Lord Jesus laid down his sweet head.
   The stars in the bright sky looked down where he lay,
   The little Lord Jesus asleep on the hay.

2. The cattle are lowing, the baby awakes,
   But little Lord Jesus, no crying he makes.
   I love thee, Lord Jesus, look down from the sky,
   And stay by my cradle till morning is nigh.

3. Be near me Lord Jesus, I ask thee to stay
   Close by me forever, and love me, I pray.
   Bless all the dear children in thy tender care,
   And fit us for heaven to live with thee there.

The Holly and the Ivy

Traditional English carol

The hol - ly and the i - vy, When they are both full grown, Of__ all the trees that are in the wood The__ hol - ly bears the crown. The ris - ing of the sun,__ And the run-ning of the deer, The__ play-ing of the mer-ry or - gan, Sweet sing-ing in the choir.

1. The holly and the ivy,
   When they are both full grown,
   Of all the trees that are in the wood
   The holly bears the crown.

   Chorus:
   The rising of the sun,
   And the running of the deer,
   The playing of the merry organ,
   Sweet singing in the choir.

2. The holly bears a blossom
   As white as the lily flower,
   And Mary bore sweet Jesus Christ
   To be our sweet Savior:

   Chorus

3. The holly bears a berry
   As red as any blood,
   And Mary bore sweet Jesus Christ
   To do poor sinners good:

   Chorus

4. The holly bears a prickle
   As sharp as any thorn,
   And Mary bore sweet Jesus Christ
   On Christmas Day in the morn:

   Chorus

5. The holly bears a bark
   As bitter as any gall,
   And Mary bore sweet Jesus Christ
   For to redeem us all:

   Chorus

6. The holly and the ivy,
   When they are both full grown,
   Of all the trees that are in the wood
   The holly bears the crown.

   Chorus

What Child Is This?

William C. Dix, 1837–1898

Traditional English tune

What child is this, ___ who, laid to rest, ___ On

Mar - y's lap ___ is sleep - ing? Whom an - gels greet ___ with

an - thems sweet, ___ While shep - herds watch ___ are keep - ing?

1. What child is this, who, laid to rest,
   On Mary's lap is sleeping?
   Whom angels greet with anthems sweet,
   While shepherds watch are keeping?

   Refrain:
   This, this is Christ the King,
   Whom shepherds guard and angels sing:
   Haste, haste to bring him laud,
   The babe, the son of Mary.

2. Why lies he in such mean estate
   Where ox and ass are feeding?
   Come, have no fear, God's son is here,
   His love all loves exceeding.

   Refrain:
   Nails, spear, shall pierce him through,
   The cross be borne for me, for you:
   Hail, hail, the Savior comes,
   The babe, the son of Mary.

3. So bring him incense, gold, and myrrh,
   All tongues and peoples own him.
   The King of kings salvation brings,
   Let every heart enthrone him:

   Refrain:
   Raise, raise your song on high
   While Mary sings a lullaby;
   Joy, joy for Christ is born,
   The babe, the son of Mary.

God Rest You Merry, Gentlemen

William Sandy's *Christmas Carols Ancient and Modern*, 1833

Traditional English tune

O Come, O Come, Emmanuel

Latin, 9th century

Adapted from plainsong by Thomas Helmore, 1811–1890

Translation: John M. Neale, 1818–1866 (stanzas 1,2);
Henry S. Coffin, 1877–1954 (stanzas 3,4)

1. God rest you merry, gentlemen,
   Let nothing you dismay,
   For Jesus Christ our Savior
   Was born upon this day,
   To save us all from Satan's power
   When we were gone astray:

   Refrain:
   O tidings of comfort and joy,
   Comfort and joy,
   O tidings of comfort and joy,

2. In Bethlehem in Jewry
   This blessèd babe was born
   And laid within a manger
   Upon this blessèd morn;
   The which his mother, Mary,
   Nothing did take in scorn:

   Refrain

3. From God, our heavenly Father,
   A blessèd angel came,
   And unto certain shepherds
   Brought tidings of the same,
   How that in Bethlehem was born
   The Son of God by name:

   Refrain

4. "Fear not," then said the angel,
   "Let nothing you affright;
   This day is born a Savior
   Of virtue, power, and might;
   So frequently to vanquish all
   The friends of Satan quite":

   Refrain

5. The shepherds at those tidings
   Rejoicèd much in mind
   And left their flocks a-feeding
   In tempest, storm, and wind
   And went to Bethlehem straightway
   This blessèd babe to find:

   Refrain

6. But when to Bethlehem they came
   Whereat this infant lay,
   They found him in a manger
   Where oxen feed on hay;
   His mother Mary kneeling
   Unto the Lord did pray:

   Refrain

7. Now to the Lord sing praises,
   All you within this place,
   And with true love and brotherhood
   Each other now embrace;
   This holy tide of Christmas
   All others doth deface:

   Refrain

1. O come, O come, Emmanuel,
   And ransom captive Israel,
   That mourns in lonely exile here
   Until the Son of God appear.

   > *Refrain:*
   > Rejoice! Rejoice!
   > Emmanuel
   > Shall come to thee
   > O Israel!

2. O come, thou Dayspring, come and cheer
   Our spirits by thine advent here;
   Disperse the gloomy clouds of night,
   And death's dark shadows put to flight.

   > *Refrain*

3. O come, thou Wisdom from on high
   And order all things, far and nigh;
   To us the path of knowledge show,
   And cause us in her ways to go.

   > *Refrain*

4. O come, Desire of nations, bind
   All peoples in one heart and mind;
   Bid envy, strife, and quarrels cease;
   Fill the whole world with heaven's peace.

   > *Refrain*

We Three Kings

John H. Hopkins, Jr., 1820–1891

A Virgin Most Pure

Traditional English carol

Davies Gilbert's *Some Ancient Christmas Carols, 1822*

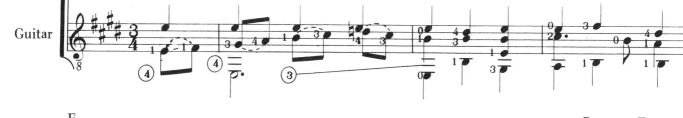

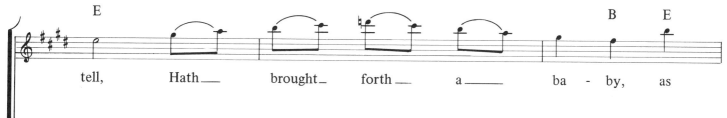

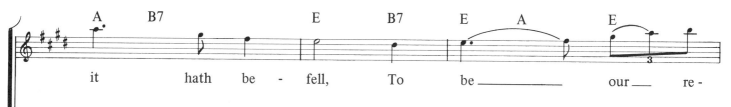

1. We three kings of Orient are
   Bearing gifts we traverse afar:
   Field and fountain, moor and mountain,
   Following yonder star.

   Refrain:
   O star of wonder, star of night,
   Star with royal beauty bright,
   Westward leading, still proceeding,
   Guide us to thy perfect light.

2. Born a king on Bethlehem's plain,
   Gold I bring to crown him again,
   King forever, ceasing never,
   Over us all to reign.

   Refrain

3. Frankincense to offer have I;
   Incense owns a deity nigh;
   Prayer and praising all men raising,
   Worship him, God on high.

   Refrain

4. Myrrh is mine: its bitter perfume
   Breathes a life of gathering gloom:
   Sorrowing, sighing, bleeding, dying,
   Sealed in a stone-cold tomb.

   Refrain

5. Glorious now behold him arise,
   King and God and sacrifice;
   Alleluia, Alleluia!
   Sound through the earth and skies.

   Refrain

1. A virgin most pure, as the prophets do tell,
   Hath brought forth a baby, as it hath befell,
   To be our redeemer from death, hell, and sin,
   Which Adam's transgression hath wrappèd us in:

   Chorus:
   Aye and therefore be merry, rejoice and be you merry,
   Set sorrows aside;
   Christ Jesus our Savior was born on this tide.

2. At Bethlehem in Jewry a city there was
   Where Joseph and Mary together did pass,
   And there to be taxèd with many one more,
   For Caesar commanded the same should be so:

   Chorus

3. But when they had entered the city so fair,
   A number of people so mighty was there
   That Joseph and Mary, whose substance was small,
   Could find in the inn there no lodging at all:

   Chorus

4. Then were they constrained in a stable to lie,
   Where the horses and asses they used for to tie;
   Their lodging so simple they took it no scorn:
   But against the next morning our Savior was born:

   Chorus

5. The King of all kings to this world being brought,
   Small store of fine linen to wrap Him was sought;
   And when she had swaddled her young son so sweet,
   Within an ox-manger she laid Him to sleep:

   Chorus

6. Then God sent an angel from heaven so high
   To certain poor shepherds in fields where they lie,
   And bade them no longer in sorrow to stay,
   Because that our Savior was born on this day:

   Chorus

7. Then presently after the shepherds did spy
   A number of angels that stood in the sky;
   They joyfully talkèd, and sweetly did sing
   To God be all glory, our Heavenly King:

   Chorus

Good King Wenceslas

John M. Neale, 1818–1866

Theodoricus Petrus of Nyland's *Piae Cantiones*, 1592

Coventry Carol

Robert Croo's *Pageant of the Shearmen and Tailors,* 1534

Original tune of 1591

Introduction or interlude

Refrain

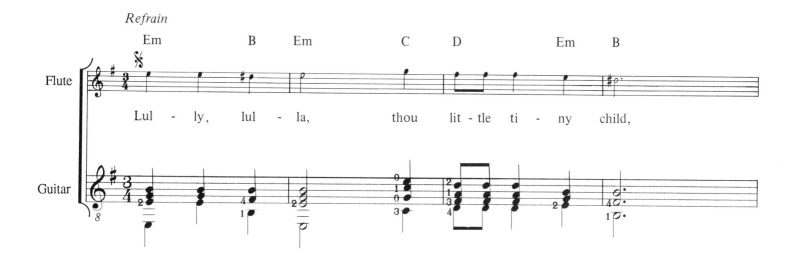

Lul - ly, lul - la, thou lit - tle ti - ny child,

1. Good King Wenceslas looked out
   On the feast of Stephen,
   When the snow lay round about,
   Deep, and crisp, and even:
     Brightly shone the moon that night
     Though the frost was cruel,
     When a poor man came in sight,
     Gath'ring winter fuel.

2. "Hither, page, and stand by me,
   If thou knowest it, telling:
   Yonder peasant, who is he?
   Where and what his dwelling?"
     "Sire, he lives a good league hence
     Underneath the mountain,
     Right against the forest fence
     By Saint Agnes' fountain."

3. "Bring me flesh, and bring me wine,
   Bring me pine logs hither:
   You and I will see him dine,
   When we bear them thither."
     Page and monarch, forth they went,
     Forth they went together;
     Through the rude wind's wild lament
     And the bitter weather.

4. "Sire, the night is darker now,
   And the wind blows stronger;
   Fails my heart, I know not how;
   I can go no longer."
     "Mark my footsteps, good my page;
     Tread thou in them boldly:
     Thou shalt find the winter's rage
     Freeze thy blood less coldly."

5. In his master's steps he trod
   Where the snow lay dinted;
   Heat was in the very sod
   Which the saint had printed.
     Therefore, Christian men, be sure,
     Wealth or rank possessing,
     Ye who now will bless the poor,
     Shall yourselves find blessing.

When a poor man came in sight, Gath-'ring win-ter fu - el.

Interlude

Refrain:
Lully, lulla, thou little tiny child,
By by, lully lullay.

1. O sisters too,
   How may we do,
   For to preserve this day,
   This poor youngling,
   For whom we do sing,
   By by, lully lullay.

   Refrain

2. Herod, the king,
   In his raging,
   Chargèd he hath this day
   His men of might,
   In his own sight,
   All young children to slay.

   Refrain

3. That woe is me
   Poor child for thee!
   And ever morn and day,
   For thy parting,
   Neither say nor sing,
   By by, lully lullay!

   Refrain

Angelus Ad Virginum

(Gabriel to Mary Came)

14th century carol

Ga - bri - el to Mar - y came, And en - tered at__ her dwell - ing
With his sal - u - ta - tion glad Her maid - en fears_ dis -

pel - ling, All hail, thou queen of vir - gins bright! God, Lord of

earth and heav- en's height, Thy_ ver - y Son shall soon be born_ in

In Dulci Jubilo

14th century German carol

1. Gabriel to Mary came, And entered at her dwelling,
   With his salutation glad Her maiden fears dispelling,
       All hail, thou queen of virgins bright!
       God, Lord of earth and heaven's height,
   Thy very Son shall soon be born in pureness
   The Savior of mankind,
       Thou art the gate of heaven bright,
       The sinner's healer kind.

2. How could I a mother be That am to man a stranger?
   How should I my strong resolve, My solemn vows endanger?
       Pow'r from the Holy Ghost on high
       Shall bring to pass this mystery,
   Then have no fear: Be of good cheer,
   Believing that still thy chastity
       In God's almighty keeping
       Shall all unsullied be.

3. Then to him the maid replied, With noble mien supernal,
   Lo! the humble handmaid I Of God the Lord eternal!
       With thee, bright messenger of heav'n,
       By whom this wondrous news is giv'n,
   I well agree and long to see
   Fulfilled thy gracious prophecy.
       As God, my Lord, doth will it,
       So be it unto me!

4. Hail! thou Mother of the Lord, Who bring'st of gifts the rarest,
   Peace to angels and to men, when Christ the Lord thou bearest!
       Do thou, we pray, entreat thy son
       For us our long'd redemption
   Himself to win, and from our sin release us;
   His succor for to give,
       That, when we hence are taken,
       We too in heaven may live.

1. *Angelus ad virginem Subintrans in conclave,*
   Virginis formidinem Demulcens, inquit, "Ave!
       Ave, regina virginum;
       Coeli terraque Dominum
   Concipies Et paries Intacta
   Salutem hominum;
       Tu porta coeli facta,
       Medela criminum."

2. *"Quomodo conciperem Quae virum non cognovi?*
   Qualiter infringerem Quod firma mente vovi?"
       "Spiritus Sancti gratia
       Perficiet haec omnia;
   Ne timeas, Sed gaudeas, Secura
   Quod castimonia
       Manebit in te pura
       Dei potentia."

3. *Ad haec virgo nobilis Respondens inquit ei:*
   "Ancilla sum humilis Omnipotentis Dei.
       Tibi coelesti nuntio,
       Tanti secreti conscio,
   Consentiens, Et cupiens Videre
   Factum quod audio;
       Parata sum parere,
       Dei consilio."

4. *Eia mater Domini, Quae pacem reddidisti;*
   Angelis et homini, Cum Christum genuisti;
       Tuum exora filium
       Ut se nobis propitium
   Exhibeat, Et deleat Peccata:
   Praestans auxilium
       Vita frui beata
       Post hoc exilium.

50

1. *In dulci jubilo,*
   Let us our homage shew;
   Our heart's joy reclineth
   In praesepio,
     And like a bright star shineth,
       Matris in gremio,
   Alpha es et O,
   Alpha es et O.

2. *O Jesu parvule!*
   I yearn for thee alway!
   Hear me, I beseech thee,
   O puer optime!   My prayer, let it reach thee,
       O Princeps gloriae!
   Trahe me post te!
   Trahe me post te!

3. *O Patris caritas,*
   O Natilentias!
   Deeply were we stainèd
   Puer nostra crimina;
     But thou hast for us gainèd
       Coelorum gaudia.
   O that we were there!
   O that we were there!

4. *Ubi sunt gaudia,*
   If they be not there?
   There are angels singing
   Nova cantica,
     And there the bells are ringing
       In Regis curia:
   O that we were there!
   O that we were there!

Down in Yon Forest

Traditional English carol

Introduction or interlude

Interlude or coda

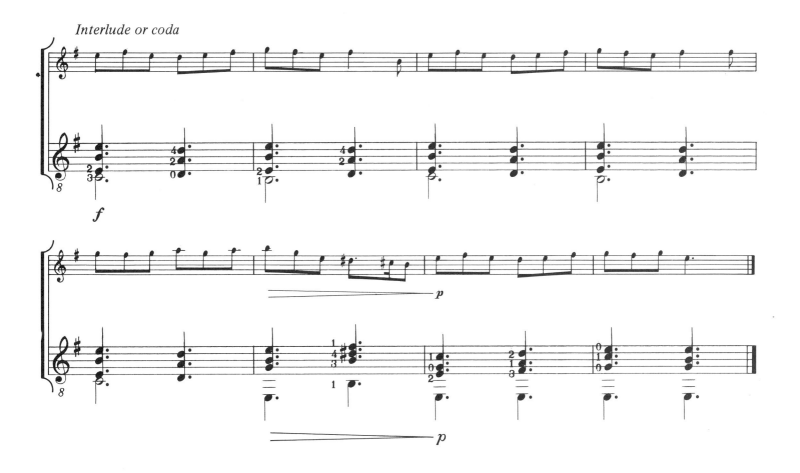

1. Down in yon forest there stands a hall:
       The bells of paradise I heard them ring;
   It's covered all over with purple and pall:
       And I love my Lord Jesus above anything.

2. In that hall there stands a bed:
       The bells of paradise I heard them ring;
   It's covered all over with scarlet so red:
       And I love my Lord Jesus bove anything.

3. At the bedside there lies a stone:
       The bells of paradise I heard them ring;
   Which the sweet virgin Mary knelt upon:
       And I love my Lord Jesus above anything.

4. Under that bed there runs a flood:
       The bells of paradise I heard them ring;
   The one half runs water, the other runs blood:
       And I love my Lord Jesus above anything.

5. At the bed's foot there grows a thorn:
       The bells of paradise I heard them ring;
   Which ever blows blossom since he was born:
       And I love my Lord Jesus above anything.

6. Over that bed the moon shines bright:
       The bells of paradise I heard them ring;
   Denoting our Savior was born:
       And I love my Lord Jesus above anything.

Hark! The Herald Angels Sing

Charles Wesley, 1707–1788

Felix Mendelssohn Bartholdy, 1809–1847

Hark ! the her - ald an - gels sing,____

"Glo - ry to the new - born King;

Peace on earth and mer - cy mild,____

God and sin - ners rec - on - ciled!"

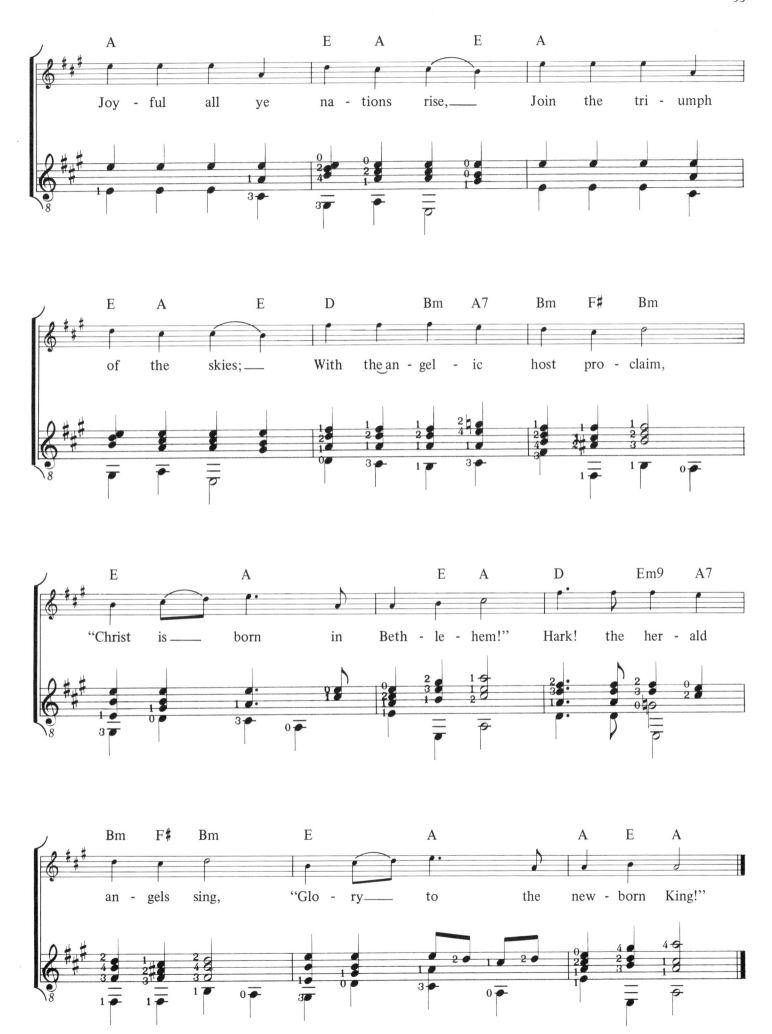

1. Hark! the herald angels sing,
    "Glory to the newborn King;
    Peace on earth and mercy mild,
    God and sinners reconciled!"
        Joyful all ye nations rise,
        Join the triumph of the skies;
        With the angelic host proclaim,
        "Christ is born in Bethlehem!"
    Hark! the herald angels sing,
    "Glory to the newborn King!"

2. Christ by highest heaven adored;
    Christ, the everlasting Lord!
    Late in time behold him come,
    Offspring of the virgin's womb.
        Veiled in flesh the Godhead see;
        Hail the incarnate Deity,
        Pleased as man with man to dwell,
        Jesus, our Emmanuel.
    Hark! the herald angels sing,
    "Glory to the newborn King!"

3. Hail the heaven-born Prince of Peace!
    Hail the Sun of Righteousness!
    Light and life to all he brings
    Risen with healing in his wings.
        Mild he lays his glory by,
        Born that man no more may die,
        Born to raise the sons of earth,
        Born to give them second birth.
    Hark! the herald angels sing,
    "Glory to the newborn King!"